Glenna
Best wishes to
you always
Pamela
July 94

The Nightingale and the Wind

For my children Zachary, Naomi, and Nicolas – P.M.

For my dearest Patrick, Amanda, Emily, Eliza, and Jane – P.S-P.

•

First published in the United States of America in 1994 by
Rizzoli International Publications, Inc.
300 Park Avenue South, New York, New York 10010
Text copyright © 1994 Paul Mandelstein
Illustrations copyright © 1994 Pamela Silin-Palmer
Compilation copyright © 1994 Rizzoli International Publications, Inc.

Library of Congress Cataloging-in-Publication Data
Mandelstein, Paul. Nightingale and the Wind / by Paul Mandelstein;
illustrated by Pamela Silin-Palmer. p. cm. Summary: With the aid of the wise Wind,
Nightingale escapes its captivity and Falcon learns a lesson in love. ISBN 0-8478-1787-3
[1. Fairy tales. 2. Nightingales-Fiction 3. Falcons-Fiction. 4. Love-Fiction.]
I. Silin-Palmer, Pamela, ill. II. Title PZ8.M325Ni 1994 [E]–dc20 93-31056

Editor: Lois Brown
Design by Patrick Palmer
Printed in Hong Kong

The Nightingale and the Wind

PAUL MANDELSTEIN

Illustrations by
PAMELA SILIN - PALMER

RIZZOLI
NEW YORK

IN ANOTHER TIME long ago, the world was ruled by the four elements of nature. These elements were known as Earth, Wind, Water, and Fire. This is a story about the Wind.

AS THE WIND TRAVELED THROUGH time and space, it would visit the tops of snow-covered mountains and the bottoms of deep, hidden valleys. It would breeze

through exotic tropical rain forests and storm across
the great rivers and oceans. And, while the Wind would
sometimes find itself in troubling situations, like mighty
hurricanes, it was quite satisfied with its place in
the world.

ONE DAY THE WIND HEARD A FAINT, SWEET sound coming from somewhere off in the distance. The sound was so compelling that the Wind was drawn irresistibly toward its source. As the Wind got closer, it became clear that this was a song. But although it had an enchanting melody, it was unmistakably a song of deep sadness.

The Wind followed the melody into a forest filled with tall trees, colorful flowers, fragrant lily ponds, and many wonderful birds and animals. And it was there, in a small clearing, that the Wind discovered the source of this magical sound. It was coming from a little Nightingale.

A feeling of great wonder stirred within the Wind. Why was this little bird's lovely song so full of sadness? Why? asked the Wind.

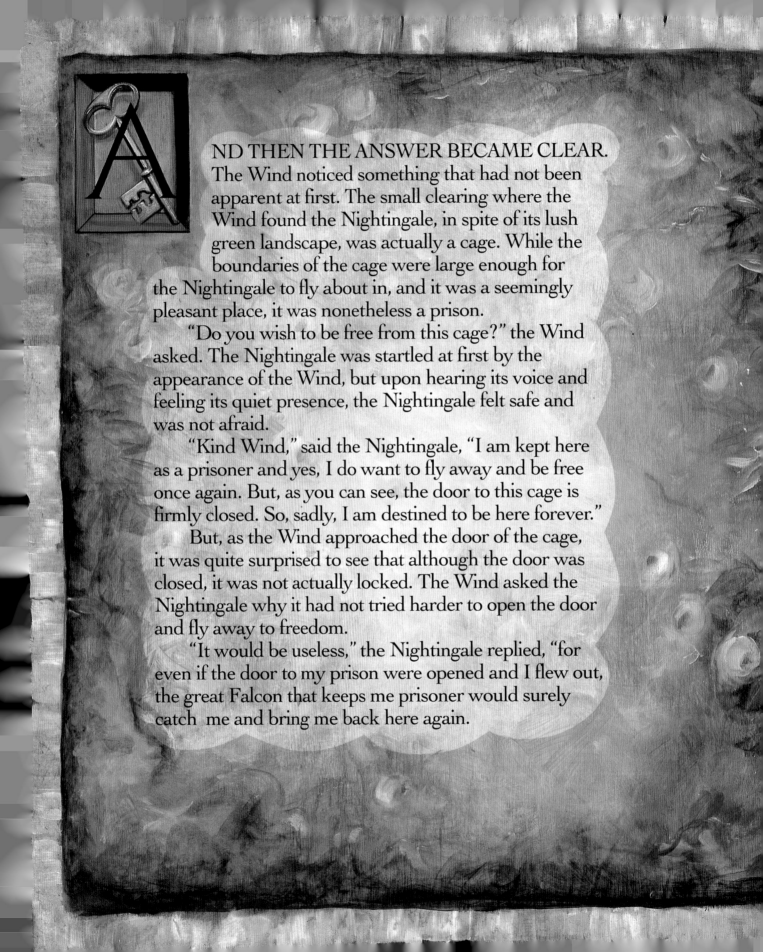

ND THEN THE ANSWER BECAME CLEAR. The Wind noticed something that had not been apparent at first. The small clearing where the Wind found the Nightingale, in spite of its lush green landscape, was actually a cage. While the boundaries of the cage were large enough for the Nightingale to fly about in, and it was a seemingly pleasant place, it was nonetheless a prison.

"Do you wish to be free from this cage?" the Wind asked. The Nightingale was startled at first by the appearance of the Wind, but upon hearing its voice and feeling its quiet presence, the Nightingale felt safe and was not afraid.

"Kind Wind," said the Nightingale, "I am kept here as a prisoner and yes, I do want to fly away and be free once again. But, as you can see, the door to this cage is firmly closed. So, sadly, I am destined to be here forever."

But, as the Wind approached the door of the cage, it was quite surprised to see that although the door was closed, it was not actually locked. The Wind asked the Nightingale why it had not tried harder to open the door and fly away to freedom.

"It would be useless," the Nightingale replied, "for even if the door to my prison were opened and I flew out, the great Falcon that keeps me prisoner would surely catch me and bring me back here again.

The Falcon is very powerful. I am not happy here, but I am afraid I am not strong enough to escape."

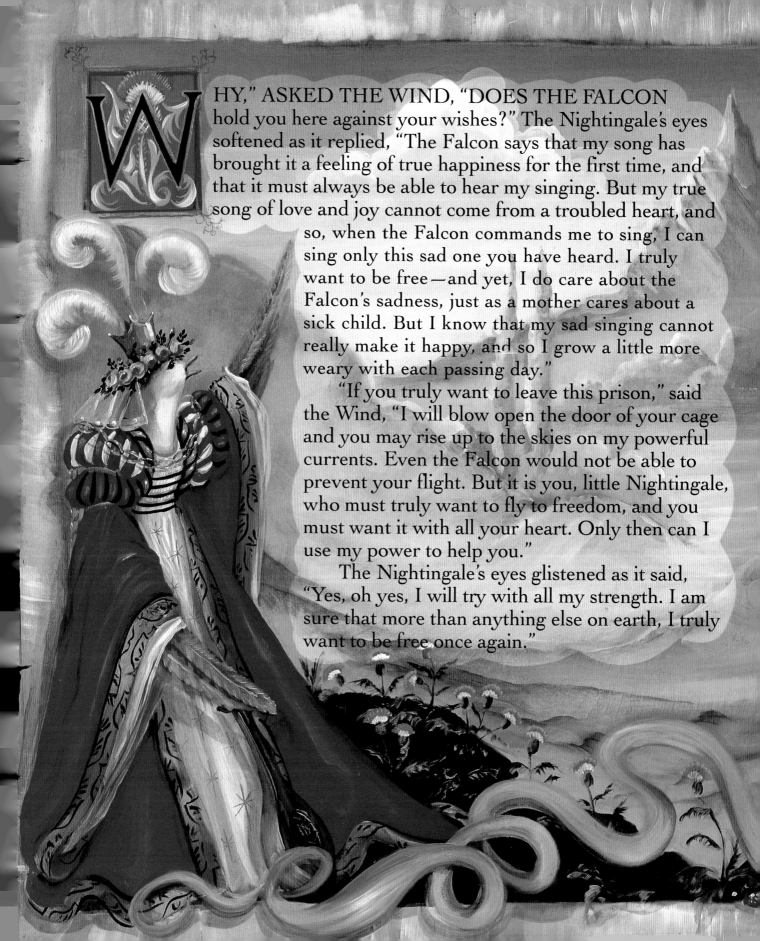

"HY," ASKED THE WIND, "DOES THE FALCON hold you here against your wishes?" The Nightingale's eyes softened as it replied, "The Falcon says that my song has brought it a feeling of true happiness for the first time, and that it must always be able to hear my singing. But my true song of love and joy cannot come from a troubled heart, and so, when the Falcon commands me to sing, I can sing only this sad one you have heard. I truly want to be free—and yet, I do care about the Falcon's sadness, just as a mother cares about a sick child. But I know that my sad singing cannot really make it happy, and so I grow a little more weary with each passing day."

"If you truly want to leave this prison," said the Wind, "I will blow open the door of your cage and you may rise up to the skies on my powerful currents. Even the Falcon would not be able to prevent your flight. But it is you, little Nightingale, who must truly want to fly to freedom, and you must want it with all your heart. Only then can I use my power to help you."

The Nightingale's eyes glistened as it said, "Yes, oh yes, I will try with all my strength. I am sure that more than anything else on earth, I truly want to be free once again."

I N THE NEXT INSTANT, WITH ALMOST NO
effort at all, the Wind blew the door to the cage wide
open. And although the Nightingale was a little unsure
that it would succeed, it flew out of the cage and headed
upward through the tall trees, aided by the currents of
the Wind.

As it flew higher, the Nightingale began to sing, and the
higher it flew the more joyful the song became. The Nightingale
was soaring with the excitement of freedom, something it had
not felt for a very long time. The higher it flew, the happier it
became.

HEN, SUDDENLY, THE LEAVES OF THE
trees began to sway and the sky turned dark.
When the Nightingale and the Wind looked up,
they saw a huge Falcon swooping toward them.
As soon as the Nightingale saw the Falcon,
it became afraid and lost its momentum, falling
backward toward the Earth. The Wind
responded quickly and, with a single breath guided the
Nightingale to safety on a low branch of a nearby tree.
The Falcon, with huge wings fully spread, descended
and settled onto a large branch just above the Nightingale.

HOW IS IT THAT YOU HAVE LEFT THE home I built for you?" demanded the Falcon angrily. "Why do you want to leave me? Destiny has brought us together, and I insist that you must stay here with me always."

The Nightingale was frightened, but feeling the Wind's presence, gathered courage and said, "It was the Wind who opened the door of my cage and set me free. The Wind heard my song and asked me about the sadness of the melody. It asked me if I wanted to be free and I said yes."

The Falcon had always been able to frighten the Nightingale—and all who entered its domain—with its angry shouting. But now it was quiet. Suddenly the Falcon began to cry, and this went on for quite some time. Then it spoke and said, "Please don't leave, little Nightingale. Though I have never cried before, the pain and emptiness that I now feel have always been with me. Hearing your song soothed my feelings of loneliness and sorrow, and filled me with happiness."

Timidly, the Nightingale replied, "I do care for you, Falcon, but the emptiness in your heart cannot be filled by my song alone; it must be filled by you. I need to be free of your cage to bring love and happiness to myself and to others."

The Falcon tossed its head and once again became very angry. "I will never free you, for if you go free I shall be empty and alone once again. I must possess you! I will never let you leave!"

THE NIGHTINGALE, while terribly frightened, took strength again from the presence of the Wind. "The Wind has freed me," the Nightingale said, "and if you really love me you'll allow me to continue my flight to freedom."

This made the Falcon furious, and the forest darkened. It screamed at the Wind, "You have tricked the Nightingale into leaving me! You are my enemy and if you do not go away immediately I will destroy you!"

"No, Falcon, I am not your enemy, and I am not frightened by your anger," the Wind replied. "For it is not I who created the pain that you feel—it was there deep inside you before I arrived. I am here only to try to help the Nightingale to gain its freedom. It is hard for you, but you must let the Nightingale go."

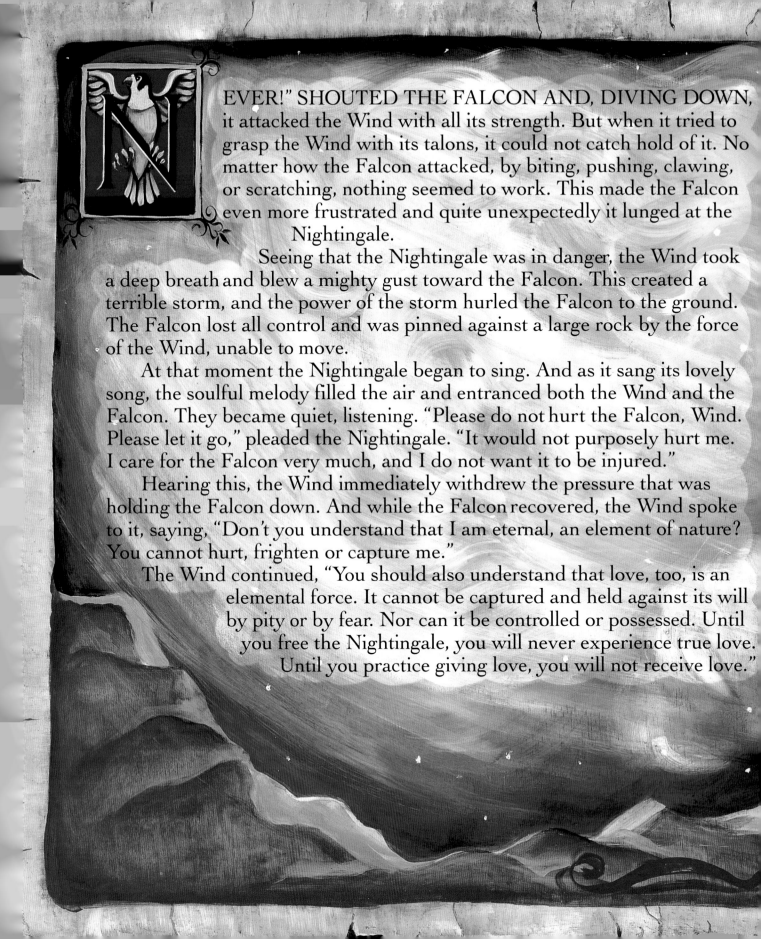

EVER!" SHOUTED THE FALCON AND, DIVING DOWN, it attacked the Wind with all its strength. But when it tried to grasp the Wind with its talons, it could not catch hold of it. No matter how the Falcon attacked, by biting, pushing, clawing, or scratching, nothing seemed to work. This made the Falcon even more frustrated and quite unexpectedly it lunged at the Nightingale.

Seeing that the Nightingale was in danger, the Wind took a deep breath and blew a mighty gust toward the Falcon. This created a terrible storm, and the power of the storm hurled the Falcon to the ground. The Falcon lost all control and was pinned against a large rock by the force of the Wind, unable to move.

At that moment the Nightingale began to sing. And as it sang its lovely song, the soulful melody filled the air and entranced both the Wind and the Falcon. They became quiet, listening. "Please do not hurt the Falcon, Wind. Please let it go," pleaded the Nightingale. "It would not purposely hurt me. I care for the Falcon very much, and I do not want it to be injured."

Hearing this, the Wind immediately withdrew the pressure that was holding the Falcon down. And while the Falcon recovered, the Wind spoke to it, saying, "Don't you understand that I am eternal, an element of nature? You cannot hurt, frighten or capture me."

The Wind continued, "You should also understand that love, too, is an elemental force. It cannot be captured and held against its will by pity or by fear. Nor can it be controlled or possessed. Until you free the Nightingale, you will never experience true love. Until you practice giving love, you will not receive love."

AT THIS POINT THE FOREST WAS SO STILL that the sound of a single leaf falling from a tree could be heard. Then all over the land a new song filled the air. At first, it was a faint, piping whistle, but it soon grew deep and strong. It was the Falcon's own love song. It was as beautiful in its own way as the Nightingale's song.

The Falcon flew about whistling this song, then after a while settled onto a branch near the Nightingale. In a softened voice it said to the Nightingale, "When you asked the Wind to release me, I realized that you really do love me! You do care about me, even though you want your freedom."

The Falcon then said to the Wind, "I know now that what you say is true." And turning to the Nightingale it said, "Dearest Nightingale, you are free to go."

At that moment, many wonderful birds and small creatures appeared. It seemed that the Wind had also blown apart all the other cages that the Falcon had built to keep the creatures it had captured. But now, sensing their safety, the freed captives happily began to fly or run to their homes and families. Some little birds and animals came and played nearby the Falcon because, knowing that it had changed in its heart, they were no longer afraid.

THE NIGHTINGALE SETTLED NEXT TO THE QUIET FALCON and said gently, "Now that you have granted me freedom to fly as I wish, and have felt kindness and love in your own heart, you will at last be able to hear and know my true song of love and joy."

"And so," continued the Nightingale, "it is time for me to fly upward into the open sky."

The Nightingale was finally free, and its song was now so beautiful that it brought tears of happiness to the eyes of all who heard it. And even today if you look skyward you may see, from time to time, a little Nightingale playing and singing joyfully on the currents of the Wind. And if you look a little harder you may even see a magnificent Falcon soaring to greater and greater heights.

THE END